Monday Popular Concerts.

DIRECTOR—Mr. S. ARTHUR CHAPPELL.

Five Hundred and Fourth Concert.*

PROGRAMME FROM THE WORKS OF

Various Masters.

MONDAY EVENING, FEBRUARY 1st, 1875.

* Nineteenth Concert of the Seventeenth Season.

Part I.

QUARTET, in B flat major, Op. 71, No. 1, for two Violins, Viola, and Violoncello. *Haydn.*

(First performance at the Popular Concerts.)

Allegro—B flat major.
Adagio—F major.
Minuetto and Trio—B flat major.
Finale, vivace—B flat major.

Madame NORMAN-NÉRUDA,

Herr L. RIES, Mr. ZERBINI, and Signor PIATTI.

(Prelude to leading theme.)

(Leading theme—melody only.)

1st Violin.

mezza voce.

&c.

(Tributary.)

&c.

pizz.

The development of this brings us, through a half close on the dominant of F, to the second theme, in that key.

(Second theme.)

(Tributary.)

Further development leads to the peroration:—

The second part, or "free *fantasia*," is entirely built upon the materials quoted. A few bars from the opening will suffice to indicate what is to follow:—

There is, however, an episode, beginning in G minor, which will hardly escape the notice of attentive listeners:—

It will be observed that two of the subsidiary themes already cited are here combined. The return to the leading theme, in the primary key, is thus brought about:—

The remainder is in the usual orthodox order, a reference to the leading theme, with a new kind of accompaniment, being the characteristic features of the *coda*:—

Thus the end of the movement accords with the spirit of its commencement—as, indeed, rarely fails to be the case with any of Haydn's works.

Adagio (theme).

(Episode.)

Further citations from this graceful, but simply constructed, movement are not called for.

Minuetto.

Trio (melody only).

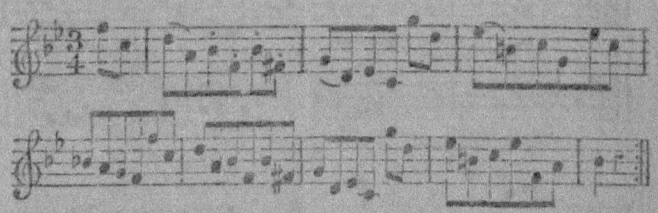

Finale (leading theme).

(Second theme.)

Cello *tacet.*

(Tributary—first violin part only.)

(Peroration—melody and bass only.)

5 K

In the second part the materials of which the first is composed are employed with the masterly skill of which Haydn has given so many examples. A very few quotations will suffice. It opens with a new and ingenious exposition of the *codetta* to the second theme :—

The themes already cited come back in due course, with the orthodox changes of key, the return of the principal subject being led up to by the most important episode :—
(Melody and bass only).

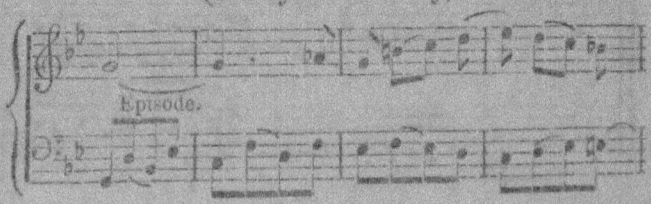

Further quotations are uncalled for. The *coda* begins as follows :—

(First violin part only).

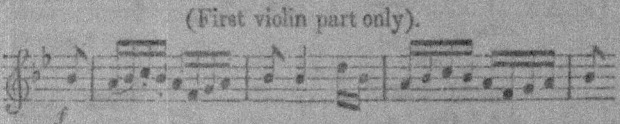

—and thus (commencing on a tonic pedal) brings this animated movement to an end, *pianissimo* :—

Both parts, according to the composer's direction, should be repeated.

Francis Joseph Haydn was born on the 21st of March, 1732, at Rhorau, and died on the 31st of May, 1809,[*] at Vienna, in his 79th year. Long as he lived, his productions are so numerous that they might reasonably account for a still more protracted career. The catalogue of his works which he drew up with his own hand, and presented to Carpani for the *Memoirs*, comprises upwards of eight hundred compositions of more or less importance. Besides his oratorios and masses, so well known to all musicians and amateurs in this country, Haydn composed twenty-four operas, one hundred and eighteen orchestral symphonies, and eighty-three quartets for stringed instruments. If he had written nothing but his quartets, he would have done quite enough—without oratorio, mass, opera, symphony, or canzonet—to render himself immortal. The number of his compositions for the chamber is prodigious, and as a whole they constitute one of the most varied and precious bequests to the art. They are otherwise interesting, moreover, for two special reasons; first, because the earlier examples exercised an undoubted influence in directing the studies and in forming the genius of Mozart; and, secondly, because the best of them show an ambition on the part of one who had been the model, and in a certain sense the master, to emulate the greatness of his still more gifted pupil and successor. It is an incident unique in the history of music, that Haydn, to whom Mozart owed so much, should afterwards have repaid himself with interest, by borrowing from the very source to which he had originally contributed. Every amateur knows what Mozart thought of Haydn; and every amateur equally knows what Haydn thought of Mozart.

---

[*] The year of Mendelssohn's birth, and fifty years subsequent to the death of Handel.

ARIETTA, Miss ALICE FAIRMAN. *Beethoven.*

In questa tomba oscura,
   Lasciami riposar ;
Quando vivevo ingrata,
   Dovevi a me pensar.
Lascia che l'ombre ignude
   Godansi pace almen ;
E non bagnar miei ceneri,
   D'inutile velen.

The words of this *Arietta*, by the Abbé Carpani (who wrote the biography of Haydn), were set by many other composers besides Beethoven, but by none so expressively. A volume published by Peters, at Leipsic, contains 18 musical settings of Carpani's text ; and among other names we find those of Himmel, Hoffman, Paer, Righini, Salieri, Weigl, Sterkel, Kozeluch, and Zingarelli. A Viennese lady of noble birth, took such a fancy to the words that she had them set no less than 63 times. The title of this curious and now very rare collection is as follows—" *'In questa tomba oscura'*— *Arietta con accompagnimento di piano, composia di diverse manieri da molti autori e dedicata al Princesse Guiseppe di Lobkowitz.*" The lady herself illustrated the volume, with a caricature of an inconsolable widow, in the costume of Louis XIV, and distributed it among her friends. We look in vain for any beauties in Carpani's lines to justify an enthusiasm so singular. Beethoven's song, however, will always remain a favourite with *contralti*.

———

SUITE DE PIÈCES, in E minor, Op 72, for Pianoforte alone. *J. Raff.*

(First performance at the Popular Concerts.)

Preludio (allegro agitato)—E minor.
Minuetto—E major; with alternativo—A major.
Toccata (vivace)—C major.
Romanza (andante)—G major.
Fuga (allegro brioso)—E minor.

Dr. HANS VON BÜLOW.

A mere indication of the themes upon which the several movements of this *suite* are constructed will answer all purposes. Unlike the *suites* of the elder masters, in form as in length of development, only two of the five pieces (the prelude and fugue—the first and the last) are in the same key, and they would seem to have, except in two instances, to be pointed out, no absolute connection with each other. Nevertheless, each is individually characteristic, as will be easily seen in the brief citations of which space admits.

Preludio.

Attention should be paid to the bass part (—page 698), which is a conspicuous figure in the third and fifth movements.

Minuetto.

After the conclusion of this, the *minuetto* is repeated, *notatim.*

Toccata.

Observe the bass of the second theme of this *toccata*, and its resemblance to that of the theme of the first movement () will not escape notice:—

(Second theme.)

This *Toccata* is a veritable *moto continuo*, the semi-quavers being kept on, either in the right hand or the left, to the end.

Romanza.

The printed edition of this *Romanza* bears the super-scription—"with alterations suggested by Dr. Hans von Bülow, and adopted by the composer."

Fuga.

Compare the theme of this *fugue* with the bass passages already referred to (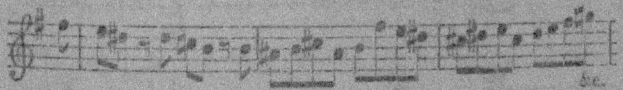) in the *Preludio* and *Toccata*, and Raff's contrapuntal ingenuity will at once be detected. Further on (as attentive hearers will hardly fail to observe) the theme is freely inverted :—

(Theme inverted.)

The counterpoint must speak for itself. Thus the *fugue* progresses with ever increasing spirit to the end.

*** Dr. HANS VON BÜLOW will perform on one of Messrs. JOHN BROADWOOD and SONS' Concert Grand Pianofortes.

SATURDAY POPULAR CONCERTS, ST. JAMES'S HALL.—On Saturday afternoon, February 6, the Programme will include Beethoven's Rasoumowski Quartet, in C major; Spohr's Pianoforte Quintet, in D minor; Grieg's Sonata, in F major, for Pianoforte and Violin; and Haydn's Air with Variations, in F minor, for Pianoforte alone. Executants, MM. HANS VON BÜLOW, SAINTON, ZERBINI, L. RIES, and PIATTI. Vocalist, Miss ELLEN HORNE. Conductor, Sir JULIUS BENEDICT. To commence at Three o'Clock.

Subscription Tickets, to the Sofa Stalls, for the 7 Morning Concerts, taking place on Saturdays, January 16, 23, 30, February 6, 13, 20, and 27, at £1 10s.

Sofa Stalls, 5s. Balcony, 3s. Admission, 1s. Tickets and Programmes at CHAPPELL & Co.'s, 50, New Bond Street.

Entr' Acte.

HERR JOACHIM RAFF.*

Herr Joachim Raff—next to Wagner himself, the most prominent orchestral writer in the band which ranges itself under the banner of that daring and powerful chief—was born at Lachen in Switzerland, on the 27th May, 1822. He began life as a schoolmaster though he appears always to have practised music. Struggling on with the true perseverance of a genuine artist, in the latter part of 1843 he was most favourably introduced by Mendelssohn to Messrs. Breitkopf & Härtel, the well-known publishers of Leipsic, all the more favourably because the motive of the act arose from no personal knowledge, but from the impression which his compositions had made on that great and genial master. We are fortunately in a position to give a copy of the letter, which, besides its testimony to Mendelssohn's anxiety to serve a rising musician, shows how voluminously Raff was already writing even at that early date :—

" Leipsic, 20th November, 1843.

" Most respected Sirs,

" I have received the enclosed letter and compositions, and cannot refrain from submitting them to you in the hope that you may be able to indulge both the writer and myself with a favourable answer to our wish. Were the pieces only signed by some well-known name I am persuaded they would have a very large sale, for the contents are such that it would be difficult to believe that many of the pieces were not by Liszt, Döhler, and other eminent players. The composition is elegant and faultless throughout, and in the most modern style ; but now comes the fact that no one knows the name of the composer, which entirely alters the case. Perhaps a single piece might be taken out of each set, or possibly you may find that one or two of those for which I personally care least (*e.g.* the Galops) are more suited for the public taste ; in a word, perhaps you may somehow be induced to print something out of the collection. If my hearty recommendation will have any weight, I most willingly add it to the request of my young friend.

---

* From the Crystal Palace Analytical Programme.—Nov. 14, 1874.

In any case I must ask you to try the pieces over, and refer them to those friends who usually advise you in such cases, and then let me know the result, returning the letter at the same time, but I trust with only a little of the music. Such is my hope, which I I beg you to pardon and excuse.

"Yours faithfully,

"F. M. B."

In 1846 Raff made Mendelssohn's personal acquaintance at Cologne, and was urged by him to complete his musical studies at Leipsic, but the scheme was frustrated by Mendelssohn's death in 1847. After a short residence in Cologne, Raff went to Stuttgart where he made the acquaintance of Herr von Bülow. Here he resided for some time, composing much music, but finding it impossible to get any of it performed; and a curious anecdote is told of Lindpaintner, the chief conductor of the Orchestra, which shows how much greater was his care for his own reputation than his desire to assist a rising brother artist. In 1849 Raff changed his abode to Weimar and then to Wiesbaden, where he has since permanently lived. His industry is something extraordinary, considering the late period at which he began his career and the size and careful finish of many of his works. If the present is a fair specimen of his orchestral works, then they are certainly remarkable, whether belonging to the very highest class or not. On the writer the Symphony makes a similar impression to that made by Victor Hugo's poetry. There is the same originality in both, the same exuberance, the same force and picturesqueness, the same love of effect, and also, it must be admitted, the same tendency to exaggeration, and the same occasional want of refinement, not to use a harsher word.

Herr Raff's published orchestral works, comprise six * Symphonies a Sinfonietta, a Suite, five Overtures, and a March; two compositions for Pianoforte and Orchestra; five String Quartets; a Quintet for Piano and Strings; four Trios for ditto, and five Sonatas for Piano and Violin. In addition, the list contains Operas and other large vocal compositions, and a host of smaller pieces numbering in all not far short of two hundred. The "interest in something new and untried" and the pleasure "in that kind of uncertainty which leaves room for the musician and the public

---

* No. 1, "Vaterland-Sinfonie" in D (obtained the prize at Vienna in 1862). No. 2, in C. No. 3, in G minor. No. 4, "Wald-Sinfonie," in F. No. 5, "Lenore," in E. No. 6, in D minor.

to have an opinion"—which Mendelssohn felt so keenly and
expressed so strongly in one of his letters to Hiller, attaches
itself in a peculiar degree to Raff's music. Much as it is
played in Germany, in England it is all but unknown. A
chamber piece or two, and a couple of movements from an
orchestral work, are all the great musical public of England
knows of a composer whose works already amount to the large
number already mentioned, and whose name is found in
almost every concert programme in his native country.

("G.")

THE LITERATURE OF THE FINE ARTS.

(*From the "Musical World."*)

The Fine Arts, truly observes the *Guide Musical*, all possess a
special literature of their own. The facts are naturally laconic;
not so the discussions arising out of matters of taste involved in
them. Many a painting covering only a small extent of canvas
has caused thousands of reams of paper to be blackened with ink,
and more than one dreamy commentator on Shakespeare, the poet
who saw—

"Sermons in stones, and good in everything,"

would be ready and willing to write a bulky folio upon every stone
to which Shakespeare may have alluded, supposing it had been sub-
jected to the Chisel of a Benvenuto Cellini, or any other sculptor
of equal or less note. When books of this description mix up
biography with criticism, and do not speak exclusively a technical
language, they may undoubtedly possess some interest for the
ordinary reader, and exert a certain influence upon the tone of
literature in general. With regard to music, however—if we except a certain number of special works, we boast of no musical biography which can attract save any musicians.

The isolation of music, with regard to the other fine arts and
to literature, is proved by the extremely rare occasion on which
we come across citations derived from it. Every day we find
writers speaking familiarly of painting, without themselves being
painters. The description of some scene or landscape serves to in-
troduce a reference to a picture or an artist; but it is far more
rarely that we meet with any allusion to the Pastoral Symphony
of Beethoven or the *Seasons* of Haydn.

That music, which exercises a more prompt, not to say a deeper,
impression on the human mind than any other art, should yet not
have supplied the language of literature with more of those happy
terms which recall it to the memory, is a fact to be explained partly
by its origin, and partly by its nature. In the first place, Music is
the youngest of the Fine Arts. At the period of the Renaissance,
poetry, painting, sculpture, and architecture, seem to have been
transmitted to us from antiquity, united and grouped together like
sister muses, each presenting mankind with material and appreci-
able results. Music, on the contrary, which, among the ancients,

was, probably, nothing more than a kind of improvised recitative did not form a portion of the group. Thus, for classic music, there was no new birth, or Renaissance: for classic music, there were no echoes of the past. It was forgotten as though it had never existed, being scarcely mentioned, even as a kind of reminiscence, by those who sought something altogether modern and original.

Musical criticism, lastly, is the most professional of all criticism: everything which, in music, is popular and unprofessional, cannot be conveyed in words; we see the products of other arts, but we feel those of music. The theory and criticism of painting are eminently picturesque: the pen of more than one pictorial critic we could name possesses all the power and all the colour of Rembrandt's brush, and poets succeed in pourtraying truthfully even that really heavenly beauty which sometimes lights up the human countenance; but we have never yet met with anyone, however eloquent he might be, capable of expressing his sensations on hearing an *adagio* of Beethoven's, except by outbursts of uniform enthusiasm—or by silence, which is, perhaps, more significant.

Despite these facts, however, we are surprised that the biography of composers should, as a rule, be so concise and so sparingly supplied with those details of private life which familiarise us with men of genius in other arts. Musicians may, not without good and sufficient grounds, be ranked among those inspired beings who sometimes speak to the soul the language of prophecy —among the interpreters of Nature and of Nature's oracles, the mysterious purport of which they alone can translate. Of all forms of power exercised by human art, that by which a great composer—

> "Seizes the soul and, in his giant grasp,
> Bears it, entranc'd and captive, unto Heav'n,"

ought to inspire us with an eager wish to learn a little of him from whom it emanates.

Nor is the history of musicians deficient in those instances of picturesque originality, and of contrasted individuality, which lend a dramatic interest to all biography. Some musical artists have played an important part in the life of nations, especially as regards social development. From John Marbeck, of Windsor, who, by his Musical Services, consoled himself and his fellow-religionists under persecution, and Marenzio, who fell a victim to a Pope's hatred, down to the composer of *Die Wacht am Rhein*, leading a people in arms to batttle and to victory; from Josquin, styled by Adami, "L'uomo insigne per l'Invenzione," down to Mendelssohn, the regenerator of Greek and of French tragedy, the world has been agitated by numerous revolutions to which Music was no stranger, and musicians were frequently actors in various scenes of this human drama. The lives of some of them are fully as remarkable and interesting as those of any of the poets.

N. V. N.

Part II.

SONATA, in A major, Op. 30, No. 1, for Pianoforte and
Violin.* *Beethoven.*

(Third performance at the Popular Concerts.)

Allegro—A major.
Adagio—D major.
Allegretto con variazioni—A major and minor.

Dr. HANS VON BÜLOW and
Madame NORMAN-NÉRUDA.

It may be interesting to know that the magnificent *presto,*
which constitutes the *finale* of the grand Sonata in A minor
(Op. 47), was not originally intended for that work, but for
the one in A major, now introduced. Beethoven, however,
conceiving it too florid and brilliant for the character of the
rest, attached it to the sonata which, though composed ex-
pressly for the young and talented English violinist, Bridge-
tower, he afterwards dedicated to Kreutzer—whose name is
rendered immortal by the inscription.

The Sonata in A major (Op. 30) is the first of a set of
three inscribed to the Russian Emperor, Alexander. The
"*Grand Aveugle*" of the day (as the *Universal Musical
Gazette of Leipsic* has been christened) does not even mention
the second of the set, the celebrated Sonata in C minor, and
is satisfied with declaring its inability to understand the first,
the one in A—as if there was anything in the slightest degree
approaching obscurity or mystification in that work, which,
from end to end, is as transparent as crystal. The other
oracle, the *Allgemeine Music-Zeitung*—which used to treat
Beethoven as *Blackwood* and *The Quarterly* used to treat
Wordsworth, Shelley, Keats, and others—criticises all three
of the sonatas (Op. 30), and the grandest of the three (in C
minor) with the least consideration. But, happily, while the
criticisms are defunct, the sonatas, still young and full of
vigorous life, are admired and praised by everyone who has a
sense of the beautiful and is capable of being impressed by its

* No. 7 of HALLÉ's edition of Beethoven's Sonatas for Pianoforte and Violin—published by CHAPPELL and Co. 50, New Bond
Street.

manifestation in harmony and melody. The one in A major, though not designed on so large a scale as other similar compositions of Beethoven, is a masterpiece of freshness, grace, and symmetry. A mere indication of the leading themes in each of the three movements will answer all purposes :—

Allegro (first theme).

(Second theme).

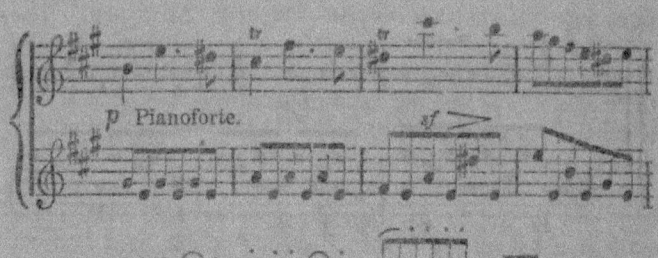

(See also the grand trio in the last scene of Meyerbeer's *Robert le Diable.*)

709

Adagio (leading theme).

Finale, allegretto (theme).

5 M

Four variations, in the major key, immediately follow the theme. The fifth variation is in the minor :—

Violin.

What is styled the "sixth variation" is really no variation at all, but a merry and graceful *coda*. The first few bars are subjoined :—

The three sonatas for pianoforte and violin, Op. 30, were composed in 1802, and dedicated to the Russian Emperor, Alexander.

The Sonata in A major was first introduced by Madame Arabella Goddard and Herr Becker, at the fourteenth concert of the second season—March 5, 1860.

SONG, Miss ALICE FAIRMAN.* *Schubert.*

DER NEUGIERIGE.

Ich frage keine Blume,
  Ich frage keinen Stern;
Sie können mir alle nicht sagen,
  Was ich erführ so gern.
Ich bin ja auch kein Gärtner,
  Die Sterne stehn zu hoch,
Mein Bächlein will ich fragen
  Ob mich mein Herz belog.

O Bächlein, meiner Liebe,
  Wie bist du heut so stumm?
Will ja nur Eines wissen,
  Ein Wörtchen um und um?
"Ja," heisst das eine Wörtchen,
  Das andre heisset "nein."
Die beiden Wörtchen schliessen
  Die ganze Welt mir ein.

O Bächlein, meiner Liebe,
  Was bist du wunderlich?
Will's "ja" nicht weiter sagen,
  Sag', Bächlein, liebt sie mich?

THE QUESTION.

I question no sweet flower,
  I question no fair star;
They all have nought to tell me,
  From them my thoughts are far.
I also am no gard'ner,
  The stars all stand too high;
My brooklet will I question
  If happiness is nigh.

O brooklet, that I dearly love,
  Why art thou silent still?
I long for only one word,
  One word my heart will fill!
"Yes" is the name of one word,
  The other is call'd "no;"
And these two words encircle
  The whole sweet world I know!

O brooklet, that I love so well,
  Why dost not speak to me?
Wilt "yes" not to me answer?
  Say, brooklet, loves she me?

This is No. 6 of a Collection of Songs by Schubert, entitled "The fair Maid of the Mill" (*Die schöne Müllerin*). The words of Müller are translated into English by Clarina Macfarren.

* Published by CHAPPELL and Co. 50, New Bond Street.

AN INTERVAL OF FIVE MINUTES.

TRIO, No. 3, in A minor, Op. 124, for Pianoforte, Violin, and Violoncello. *Spohr.*

(Second performance at the Popular Concerts.)

Allegro moderato—A minor and major.
Andante con variazioni—F major.
Scherzo—D minor; with Trio—D major.
Presto—A minor and major.

Dr. HANS VON BÜLOW,

Madame NORMAN-NERUDA, and Signor PIATTI.

The Trio in A minor (No. 3), like the Trio in F major (No. 2), its immediate predecessor, was composed at Cassel in the year 1842. Each movement is of that plain, straightforward character that a few brief quotations will answer all purposes.

Allegro moderato (leading theme).

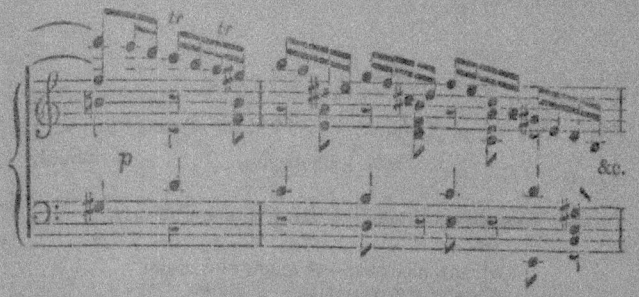

(Second theme—C major.)

Andante (theme).

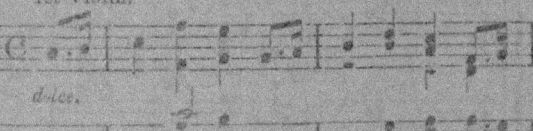

The development of this melody, in the variation form, and the brilliant pianoforte accompaniment, which is a special feature, will speak for themselves.

Scherzo (melody only).

Violin and Cello.

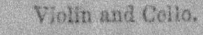

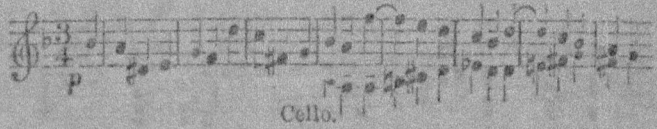

Cello.

Trio (melody and bass only).

Finale (theme).

(Second theme—C major.)

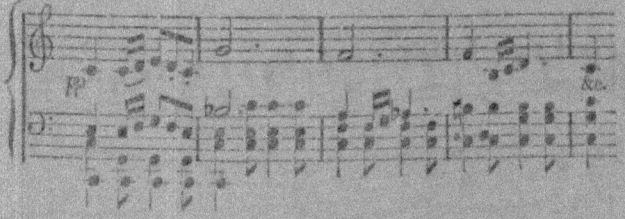

This is associated with a brilliant pianoforte accompaniment, after the subjoined pattern :—

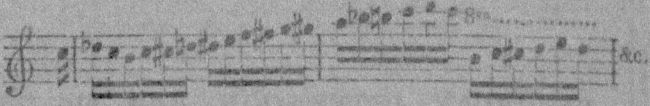

Further quotations are not called for.

In the *Selbst-Biographie*, a bare reference to the second and third of Spohr's pianoforte trios is all that is to be found. About the first, however—the one in E minor—the following appreciation is cited from the *Leipziges Neue Zeitschrift* :—

"Although the great master has never written anything of this kind until now, he moves with true artistic consciousness of power and with genial freedom. The trio is one of the finest productions of the genius of Spohr, the greatest possible symmetry of form being combined with a profusion of beauties and master-strokes of genius, standing out in prominent relief. As the gem of the whole, the *scherzo*, with its attendant *trio*, must be named. Here, as though in obedience to the wand of a musician, a fairy island of the blessed is conjured up by the imagination. We are surrounded as though by a garden of wonders, a blooming oasis of sound, full of the deep glowing splendour of oriental colour! . . . It is extraordinary how Spohr has been able to combine two elements, strange, and, indeed, normally antagonistic the one to the other—the humoristic element and the impassioned, elegiacally tender element, &c."

The foregoing may be accepted *bonâ fide*, but *cum grano salis*.

The Trio in A minor was first introduced by Dr. Hans von Bülow, Herr Straus, and Signor Piatti, at the third concert of the seventeeth season.—*Nov.* 16, 1874.

END OF THE FIVE HUNDRED AND FOURTH

CONCERT.

J. MALLETT, PRINTER, 59, WARDOUR STREET, SOHO, LONDON. W.

SATURDAY POPULAR CONCERTS.

SATURDAY AFTERNOON, FEB. 6th, 1875.

PROGRAMME.

QUARTET, in C major, Op. 59, No. 3, for two Violins,
Viola, and Violoncello ....*Beethoven.*
MM. SAINTON, L. RIES, ZERBINI, and PIATTI.

SONG, "Name the glad day" ....*Dussek.*
Miss ELLEN HORNE.

FANTASIEBILDER, Op. 26, for Pianoforte alone............*Schumann.*
(First time at the Popular Concerts.)
Dr. HANS VON BÜLOW.

SONATA, in F major, for Pianoforte and Violin ....*Grieg.*
(First time at the Popular Concerts.)
Dr. HANS VON BÜLOW and M. SAINTON.

SONG, "Pack, clouds, away" ....*G. A. Macfarren.*
Miss ELLEN HORNE.
Clarionet obbligato, Mr. LAZARUS.

QUINTET, in D minor, Op. 130, for Pianoforte, two Violins,
Viola, and Violoncello ....*Spohr.*
Dr. HANS VON BÜLOW,
MM. SAINTON, L. RIES, ZERBINI, and PIATTI.

Conductor - - Sir JULIUS BENEDICT.

www.ingramcontent.com/pod-product-compliance
Lightning Source LLC
Chambersburg PA
CBHW082052220626
47052CB00006B/1220